SQUIRREL GOES SKATING

BASED ON THE STORIES BY

Alison Uttley and *Margaret Tempest*

An imprint of HarperCollins*Publishers*

Squirrel Goes Skating
was first published in 1934 by William Collins Sons & Co
This edition was first published in Great Britain by HarperCollins*Publishers* Ltd in 2000

1 3 5 7 9 10 8 6 4 2
ISBN: 0-00-710041-8

Text for this edition by Susan Dickinson based on the
television adaptation by Helen Cresswell

based on the original illustrations by Margaret Tempest.
Production of the television series by United Productions in association with Cosgrove Hall.

A CIP catalogue record for this title is available from the British Library.

The HarperCollins website address is: www.**fire**and**water**.com

Printed and bound in Hong Kong

EVERYTHING WAS FROZEN. Even the brook that ran past little Grey Rabbit's house was thick with ice. On every window were Jack Frost's pictures, trees and ferns and flowers in silver.

“Grey Rabbit! Grey Rabbit!” called Hare, as he came downstairs in his dressing gown. “Put some more wood on the fire. I believe I’ve got a chilblain. A big one! Ouch! It hurts!”

“Moldy Warp once told me to use snow to make chilblains better,” said little Grey Rabbit. “Wait.” She went outside and gathered a handful of snow to rub on Hare’s foot.

“Grey Rabbit! Grey Rabbit!” called Squirrel. “Ooh, you’ve let the North Wind in! My paw is chapped. *I* want some snow rubbed in.”

Little Grey Rabbit was rubbing Hare's foot with the soft snow when there was a knock at the door.

"Milk-o!"

Little Grey Rabbit opened the door and there stood Hedgehog, shivering on the doorstep.

"Brr. It's fruzz today," he said. And he tipped a solid chunk of milk into little Grey Rabbit's jug.

"Come in and warm yourself, Hedgehog!" said little Grey Rabbit, and she filled a saucer with hot tea. Hedgehog's feet left little puddles of water on the floor.

"Do you know there's skating over Tom Tiddler's Way? Everybody's going," he said, as he drank his tea.

"Skating!" shouted Hare. "Let's go too! Hurry up, everybody! Hurrah for skating!"

"Well, I must be getting on," said Hedgehog. "Thankee kindly for the tea."

"I'm a born skater," said Hare. "Did I ever tell you how I skated round the lily pond backwards and passed all the other skaters going forwards?"

"Some other time, Hare," said little Grey Rabbit. "We have a lot to do."

Hare went out to clean the skates. Squirrel went upstairs.

Little Grey Rabbit washed the dishes, made up the fire and cut some sandwiches.

Then she laid out a feast on the table, ready for when they came home.

At that moment Hare came back. He had a basket of icicles in his hand.

"I've been collecting these to take for drinks. You just suck one, like this, and it makes a nice watery drink."

"But you haven't changed your dressing gown," said Grey Rabbit.

"Oh, Jemima! I forgot!" exclaimed Hare, and he hurried upstairs.

"Help! Grey Rabbit! Can you come here?" called a muffled voice.

Little Grey Rabbit went up the stairs and opened the door of Squirrel's room. In the middle of the room was a green jumping dress!

"Oh, please help me!" said Squirrel. Her head was stuck in her dress and she couldn't see anything.

“Stand still a minute,” said Grey Rabbit. And she pulled the dress straight.

There stood Squirrel. She had green bows on her ears and a green bow on her tail!

“I thought we were going skating, not to the fair!” said Hare.

At last they were off. They hid the key under the snow on the windowsill. Then they ran down the lane and across the fields to Tom Tiddler's Way.

Little Grey Rabbit carried the basket with the food. Hare carried his basket of icicles and the kettle, and Squirrel carried the skates.

They passed a group of brown rabbits who nudged each other when they saw Squirrel's ribbon bows. Then Water Rat appeared. He bowed to Squirrel.

"Are you going to the fair, Miss Squirrel?" he said.

"No. I'm going skating," she replied.

"Then I will come with you." And he joined the happy group.

Soon they heard the shouts of the skaters on the ice.

Little Grey Rabbit gave her basket to Mrs Hedgehog who was sitting on a log watching her son Fuzzypeg as he slipped and slithered among the rabbits and fieldmice.

Then Squirrel, Hare and little Grey Rabbit put on their skates and joined the others on the frozen pond.

And so the fun began. Hare tried to do the outside edge and got mixed up with the skates of a white duck. Little Grey Rabbit went to help him and rubbed his bruised head with her paw. Then she saw some young brown rabbits who kept tumbling over each other. So she and Water Rat linked paws with

them and away they went, ears back, heads up, their eyes shining as their tiny feet glided over the ice.

Soon they were hungry, so they all returned to the bank and little Grey Rabbit unpacked the basket.

There was enough for all, even the crowd of hungry black-coated rooks who loitered on the pond's edge. Hare's icicles were very thin by now, but he handed round the basket, and each sucked the sweet cold ice.

After their picnic they all returned to the ice and skated until the red sun set behind the far hills and dark shadows spread across the fields.

The animals removed their skates and set off home.

"Goodbye! Goodbye!" they called. "Perhaps we'll come again tomorrow."

"Did you see me skate?" said Hare. "I did the double-outside-edge backwards, and a figure seven on one leg!"

"I saw all the little rabbits and fieldmice you knocked over!" replied Squirrel.

"Hush, both of you!" said little Grey Rabbit. "You'll wake Wise Owl."

They came to their gate. It was unlatched and there were tracks on the path.

"Someone's been here while we've been out," whispered Squirrel.

“It wasn’t the milkman, or the postman,” said Hare.

“The key’s still here,” said little Grey Rabbit, taking the key from under the snow on the windowsill.

They hurried inside. What a sight met their eyes! The table was upset, the dishes empty and overturned.

Broken pots lay on the floor and an empty bottle of primrose wine lay on its side.

“Oh, I was so hungry, and now there isn’t enough for a bumble-bee! It’s a calamity!” wailed Hare.

"Oh no, I was *so* thirsty, and there isn't a drop for a minnow!" moaned Squirrel.

"Oh! Oh! I left such a feast and now look at the dirty tablecloth and the broken dishes and the spilt wine!" said little Grey Rabbit.

"Oh, who's been here while we've been gone?" they all cried together.

A trail of dirty footprints led to the stairs. They looked at each other and slowly tiptoed up the stairs carrying their candles.

On the landing were their three bedroom doors.

Grey Rabbit cautiously peeped into her room.
"There's no one in my room," she whispered.
Hare opened his door.
"And there's no one in *my* room," he said.

Then Squirrel opened her bedroom door. There was a lump under the bedspread, a long thin tail hung over the edge of the bed and whiskers stuck out above the sheets.

"Oooh! Oooh!" squealed Squirrel. "Someone's sleeping in my bed!" The candle shook in her hand. "Who… who is it?"

"It's Rat's tail," said Hare softly.

"They're Rat's whiskers," added little Grey Rabbit.

They all crept out of the room and looked at each other in dismay.

"What shall we d… do?" said Hare.

"Let's all shoo him out together!" suggested Squirrel.

"No," said little Grey Rabbit sternly. "He ought to be punished. We ought to make him remember his wickedness."

"When I want to remember anything I tie a knot in my handkerchief," said Hare.

"I don't think Rat *has* a handkerchief," replied little Grey Rabbit.

"But he has a tail!" whispered Squirrel. "I shall tie a knot in Rat's tail and it will never, never come undone!"

They crept back into the bedroom and Squirrel picked up the long tail. She doubled it and looped it and twisted it into a great knot. Then they shut the door and ran downstairs.

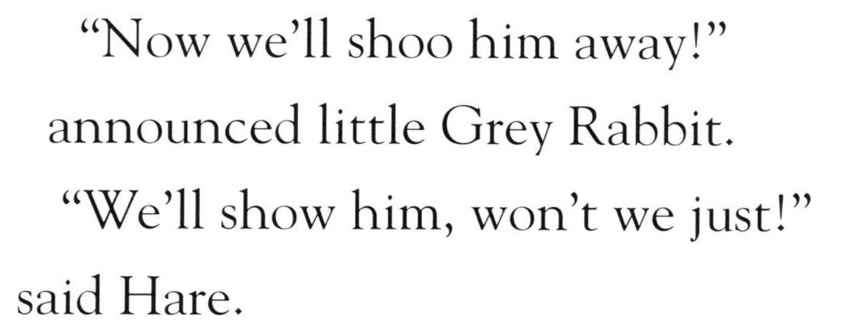

"Now we'll shoo him away!" announced little Grey Rabbit.

"We'll show him, won't we just!" said Hare.

Hare picked up the fire tongs and the poker. Little Grey Rabbit took two saucepan lids, and Squirrel picked up the bundle of skates. Then they crept back upstairs.

"Ready… Steady… Go!" shouted Hare.

They hammered and banged on the bedroom door and made such a clatter and racket that Rat woke up. He sprang out of bed, jumped out of the window, ran across the garden and away. Then he stopped.

"Whatever's that a-bumping and a-clumping behind me?" Rat twisted round and tried to unfasten the great knot in his tail, but he couldn't do it.

"Hello, Rat," said Wise Owl, as he flew overhead. "Been in mischief?"

Rat shivered and went mournfully on his way.

Little Grey Rabbit, Squirrel and Hare went downstairs to tidy up and get a warm fire going.

"Grey Rabbit! Open the door!" said a voice.

"That's Mole!" said little Grey Rabbit happily.

"We thought we'd end the skating day with a feast," said Mole, staggering in with a hamper, followed by Water Rat and the Hedgehog family.

"Hurrah!" they all cried.

And so the day's skating ended with a feast after all.